HERMY THE HERMIT CRAB
AND
THE SEA TURTLE RESCUE

BY ANDREA WEATHERS / ILLUSTRATION BY BOB THAMES

LEGACY PUBLICATIONS

HERMY THE HERMIT CRAB lived on the sandy floor of the Atlantic Ocean with all of his family and friends. They lived southwest of the barrier island called Folly— just off the coast of Charleston, South Carolina.

Hermy loved to ride the waves ashore to Folly Beach. One evening, he saw an awesome sight there. Next to a small sand dune, nearly hidden in the darkness, newly hatched sea turtles were climbing out of their sandy nest. They had just hatched from their eggshells below the surface.

They were Loggerhead Turtles, with four flippers instead of legs or fins. Each had a hard shell to protect its fragile body. As their eyes opened, the tiny turtles tried out their flippers. They pushed aside the soft sand to make their way out of the nest. Hermy saw the tiny turtles scramble in different directions.

THE HATCHLINGS BEGAN to look for the ocean, but darkness was all they saw. Hermy knew they would need the light of a full moon to help them find their new home.

One hatchling crawled toward a lavender light that glowed in the distance. The turtle thought, "Could this be the moon? Is the ocean here?" Hermy saw the tiny turtle heading the wrong way.

"No, not that way!" he warned. Hermy waved his claw and said, "Follow me."

THE TURTLE LOOKED UP at the hazy light on top of a tall wooden pole.

Hermy led the tiny turtle away from the light.

This was not the moon, only a streetlight. And there was no ocean here.

TWO HATCHLINGS WATCHED two small beams of white light coming toward them out of the darkness. The turtles thought, "Could this be the moon? Are there two moons? And is the ocean here?" Hermy saw two tiny turtles heading the wrong way.

"No, not that way!" he warned. Hermy waved his claw and said, "Follow me."

AS THE TWO LIGHTS moved closer to the hatchlings, the turtles learned that these lights were part of a giant object that rolled down the road on four wheels. Hermy led two tiny turtles away from the road.

This was not the moon, only the headlights of a car. And there was no ocean here.

THREE HATCHLINGS SPOTTED a light that was not lavender or white. This light was green. The turtles thought, "Could this be the moon? Is the ocean here?" Hermy saw three tiny turtles heading the wrong way.

"No, not that way!" he warned. Hermy waved his claw and said, "Follow me."

THE TURTLES WATCHED the green light change to bright yellow. Then the yellow light changed to red. Hermy led three tiny turtles away from the big box with three different lights in it.

This was not the moon, only a traffic light. And there was no ocean here.

FOUR HATCHLINGS HEADED toward a huge light that seemed to be coming out of the ground. It was lighting up a pale blue rectangle of water. The turtles thought, "Could this be the moon? Is the ocean here?" Hermy saw four tiny turtles heading the wrong way.

"No, not that way!" he warned. Hermy waved his claw and said, "Follow me."

A SMiLiNG LADY turned the baby turtles around. She knew that the hatchlings were in the wrong place. Hermy led four tiny turtles away from the blue light. This was not the moon, only a hotel's swimming pool. And there was no ocean here.

FIVE HATCHLINGS SPOTTED another light shining ahead. The turtles thought, "Could this be the moon? Is the ocean here?" Hermy saw five tiny turtles heading the wrong way.

"No, not that way!" he warned. Hermy waved his claw and said, "Follow me."

THE HATCHLINGS STUMBLED upon a little boy playing with his toy fire truck in the yard next to his beach house. The boy switched off the light and gently turned the young turtles around to point them toward the beach. Hermy led five tiny turtles away from the beach house.

This was not the moon, only a porch light. And there was no ocean here.

IT WAS GETTING very late and the hatchlings were becoming tired. Six hatchlings noticed six small white lights weaving down the beach toward them. The turtles thought, "Could this be the moon? Are there six moons? And is the ocean here?" Hermy saw six tiny turtles heading the wrong way.

"No, not that way!" he warned. Hermy waved his claw and said, "Follow me."

THE HATCHLINGS WATCHED a group of children run past them, holding the lights in their hands. The giggling boys and girls were following the ghost crabs scurrying sideways across the sand in search of food and water. The turtles stayed hidden in the dark. Hermy led six tiny turtles away from the moving lights.

This was not the moon, only the narrow beams of flashlights. And there was no ocean here.

SEVEN HATCHLINGS SPIED a bright orange glow in the distance. The turtles thought, "Could this be the moon? Is the ocean here?" Hermy saw seven tiny turtles heading the wrong way.

"No, not that way!" he warned. Hermy waved his claw and said, "Follow me."

THE HATCHLINGS SAW a family of people roasting marshmallows over the mysterious light. Hermy led seven tiny turtles away from the orange light, which was very hot!

This was not the moon, only the flickering flames of a campfire. And there was no ocean here.

TWENTY-EIGHT HATCHLINGS watched a yellow ball of light rise slowly above the clouds in the sky. The turtles thought, "Could this be the moon? Is the ocean here?" Hermy saw twenty-eight tiny turtles heading the *right* way.

"Yes, this way!" he exclaimed. Hermy waved his claw and said, "Follow me."

DETERMINED TO FIND the sea, the hatchlings kept going. The dry sand started to feel cool, then wet. They kept crawling toward the light that was floating even higher into the star-filled sky. Now it was turning a very bright shade of white, lighting up the shimmering waves and the entire beach.

Hermy led twenty-eight tiny turtles to the ocean.

THE HATCHLINGS WERE quite surprised when a wave
of cool water rippled over them. They made it! This big white ball of light in
the sky was the moon and this refreshing water was the ocean. The water sparkled
like silver glitter in the moonlight.

Hermy joined a small group of people standing nearby with flashlights that cast
a red glow. They all cheered for the turtles' success.

Happy with their discovery, the hatchlings paddled out to deeper water.
They joined all of the other sea turtles that hatched that evening and found their way
to the sea. One day, they would come back to the beach to lay eggs of their own.

Hermy was happy to go home and tell his family and friends about
his new adventure.

BARRIER ISLAND BEACHES have served as nesting habitats for the
Loggerhead Sea Turtle (*Caretta caretta*) for more than 150 million years. South Carolina beaches often host the Loggerhead,
and sometimes the Green Sea Turtle, the Atlantic Ridley, and the Leatherback. The nesting and hatching season takes place
May through October. The adult female sea turtle comes ashore one to four times a season and lays an average of 115 eggs.
She digs a hole in the sand, usually next to a dune, lays the eggs, covers them with sand, and goes back out to sea.

AFTER about 45 to 60 days, the hatchlings crawl out of the nest and instinctively head toward the ocean.
This usually happens at night when the temperature is cool. Sometimes, man-made lighting disorients the baby turtles. Instead of finding
their way to the sea by the light of the moon, hatchlings have been known to end up in swimming pools and at streetlights.

MANY beach communities, like Folly, Kiawah, Seabrook, Edisto, Sullivan's Island, Isle of Palms, and Hilton Head in South Carolina,
have made laws to protect the sea turtles. They want to reduce unnatural nighttime lighting from homes, motels, streetlights,
and flashlights during the turtle season. A dark beach is necessary so that the baby turtles do not waste valuable energy wandering in
the wrong direction or suffer in the sun's heat the next day. The baby turtles only have a limited amount of strength to find the
ocean and make the long 50- to 60-mile journey to the Gulf Stream and the Sargasso Sea. They will live and feed in the Gulf Stream currents
for the next few years. If a turtle does not reach this destination in about three days, it will not survive.

FOLLY has knowledgeable volunteers who walk the beach at morning's first light to look for turtle tracks. The Turtle Team,
trained by the South Carolina Department of Natural Resources, checks each nest for eggs and checks for "false crawls," or abandoned nests
with no eggs. The volunteers move any eggs that are not in safe areas, and they mark each nest and watch them until the eggs hatch.

DURING hatching time, the volunteers watch the turtles and sometimes guide them to the sea to keep them safe from ghost crabs,
people, and disorientation. After a hatch-out, the eggshells are pulled from the nest and counted to find out the number of live hatchlings.
You can see these counts and photos on the Web site www.follyturtles.com. The success rate on Folly is very good, with more than 6,000
hatchlings in 2008. It is important to have lots of hatchlings, since only about one out of 1,000 reaches adulthood.

MY story is based on actual events that happened on Folly Island. Folly has hosted many sea turtle nests over the years.
When I was growing up on the island, my mother kept us children away from the nests. We helped her guide the tiny turtles
to the sea when they mistakenly followed a streetlight or porch light on dark nights. I will always remember the sight of my younger brother,
Darrell, sitting on the concrete stoop under the porch light one evening. He was surrounded by his Matchbox cars and baby turtles.
I believe that the baby turtles we helped 40 years ago are now returning as adult turtles to nest. As long as the hatchlings
can imprint, or crawl to the water on their own so they will remember this beach, there is a good chance
that there will always be turtle nests on Folly Island.

This book is dedicated to all of the sea turtle professionals and volunteers who work diligently to preserve the species. — *AGW & RET*

Special thanks to . . .
Darrell Weathers for the inspiration for the story. For their review of the story: Sally Murphy, retired biologist, South Carolina Department of Natural Resources; Charlotte Hope, biologist, SCDNR; and Dan Evans, Caribbean Conservation Corporation.
Grey and William Gaidies for their support. And to the wonderful people at Legacy Publications!

Library of Congress Control Number: 2010929560
ISBN 978-0-933101-09-8

Legacy Publications, 1301 Carolina Street, Greensboro, NC 27401 / www.legacypublications.com
Manufactured by Friesens Corporation in Altona, MB, Canada; July 2010; Job # 56391

A BRIGHT IDEA
The light from a regular flashlight will disorient
baby turtles as well as adult turtles that come ashore to nest.
But turtles cannot see red. So before you visit the beach
at night during turtle season, it is a good idea to buy a flashlight
that has a red lens or includes a red lens cover you can attach.
If this is not available, place a piece of red cellophane
over the lens and secure it with a rubber band.
This will allow you to see the beach at night
and not distract the turtles.

THE  END